YOSSI and the MONKEYS

A Shavuot Story

D1294859

For all the sweet monkeys who make our circus
together so wonderful. — J.T.M.

To Eli, Tom, Taiyo, Leo, & Saba Gaby. — S.W.

About Shavuot

Shavuot means "weeks" in Hebrew. This holiday, called the Feast of Weeks, comes seven weeks after Passover. It celebrates the time that the Jewish people received the Torah. Shavuot also marks the harvest of the first fruits of summer. It is said that the words of Torah are as sweet as milk and honey, so it is traditional to eat dairy foods, such as blintzes, at festive meals.

Text copyright © 2017 by author Jennifer Tzivia MacLeod
Illustrations copyright © 2017 by Lerner Publishing Group.

All rights reserved. International copyright secured. No part of this book may be reproduced, stored in a retrieval system, or transmitted in any form or by any means—electronic, mechanical, photocopying, recording, or otherwise—without the prior written permission of Lerner Publishing Group, Inc., except for the inclusion of brief quotations in an acknowledged review.

KAR-BEN PUBLISHING
A division of Lerner Publishing Group, Inc.
241 First Avenue North
Minneapolis, MN 55401 USA
1-800-4-KARBEN

Website address: www.karben.com

Main body text set in Chaloops.
Typeface provided by Chank.

Library of Congress Cataloging-in-Publication Data

Names: MacLeod, Jennifer Tzivia, author. | Waisman, Shirley, illustrator.
Title: Yossi and the monkeys : a Shavuot story / by Jennifer Tzivia MacLeod ; illustrated by Shirley Waisman.
Description: Minneapolis : Kar-Ben Publishing, [2017] | Summary: "An escaped circus monkey with a talent for juggling helps Yossi sell the kippahs and vests his wife makes and to earn enough money to celebrate Shavuot with his family"—Provided by publisher.
Identifiers: LCCN 2016009546 (print) | LCCN 2016029274 (ebook) | ISBN 9781467789325 (lb : alk. paper) | ISBN 9781467794213 (pb : alk. paper) | ISBN 9781512427219 (eb pdf)
Subjects: | CYAC: Shavuot—Fiction. | Monkeys—Fiction.
Classification: LCC PZ7.1.M246 Yo 2017 (print) | LCC PZ7.1.M246 (ebook) | DDC [E]—dc23

LC record available at https://lccn.loc.gov/2016009546

Manufactured in the United States of America
1-38118-19962-6/6/2016

YOSSI and the MONKEYS
A Shavuot Story

Jennifer Tzivia MacLeod

illustrated by
Shirley Waisman

KAR-BEN
PUBLISHING

Shavuot was coming, but Yossi had no money for braided challahs or blintzes for the children, let alone flowers for his wife, Malka.

"Perhaps we can sell something in the market," Malka said.

"What a good idea! How about kippahs like mine?" Yossi said, holding up the one she'd made for him.

So with the last of her fabric, Malka made three beautiful kippahs that shone with the colors of the rainbow.

Off went Yossi, whistling into town with the kippahs in a basket. But nobody wanted to buy kippahs.

Discouraged, Yossi sat down
to rest beneath a tree.

When he woke up,
the kippahs were gone!

SNAP! The sound came from the branches above. Yossi looked up and saw a monkey— wearing a kippah and juggling the two others!

"Give those back!" Yossi called.

But the monkey just swung through the trees, leaping from branch to branch with the kippahs.

A man stopped to stare at the monkey.
"Are those your kippahs?" he asked Yossi.
"How much is that one?"

"Um . . . one ruble?" said Yossi hesitantly.

The man held out two rubles. "One more for
your monkey, who made me smile."

The monkey handed over the kippah
with a bow.

"Look, a monkey!" called a boy.

His mother laughed. "How much for the purple kippah?"

"One ruble," said Yossi.

The monkey held out the purple kippah and bowed.

On the way home, Yossi passed the fruit stand.
The monkey began to rub his belly.

"What can I buy with half a ruble?" he asked the fruit seller.

The fruit seller handed Yossi an apple.

The monkey polished the apple on his fur and nibbled. Then he reached out and touched Yossi's hand. A warm feeling came over Yossi.

"Thank you . . . Zelig," Yossi said, giving the monkey a name. "'Zelig' means 'blessing' and you are my blessing."

With some of the rubles,
Yossi bought vegetables for soup
for his children.

With some of the rubles, Malka bought
fabric. She sewed more kippahs and even
some colorful vests.

And beneath his pillow, Yossi
hid two coins to buy Shavuot
flowers for his wife.

For three days, Yossi went into the town square with Zelig. Zelig danced, tossing the kippahs like a juggler. Coins jingled as people bought kippahs.

And each evening Zelig sat on Yossi's shoulder to munch his apple before vanishing into the treetops.

Then came a rainy day.
And another.

On the third day, when the rain finally stopped, Yossi rushed outside. "Zelig!" he called. But there was no Zelig.

Yossi spotted a poster: *A circus!* Could Zelig be there? A ticket cost seven rubles.

Yossi ran to the largest house in town and knocked on the door.

"No kippahs today," the woman said.

"How about a vest for Hershele?" He held up one just her son's size. "Fit for a king—for Shavuot, the birthday of King David himself! Yours for just seven rubles!"

She paid Yossi and took the vest. Yossi hurried along to the circus.

Inside the tent, the crowd murmured
excitedly. A man in a top hat appeared.

"Ladies and gentleman," he began, "our
monkeys will **not** be performing . . ."
But then people began giggling.

Behind the manager, out crept a
monkey. **Zelig!**

The monkey leaped up on a wire, bounded over the seats, and landed on Yossi's shoulder.

"You!" shouted the manager. "Give me back my monkey!"

With Zelig on his shoulder, Yossi followed the angry manager out of the ring.

"You've ruined my monkey!" the manager yelled. "He won't do what I say! And all the other monkeys do whatever **he** does."

Yossi shrugged. "He was hungry. I gave him apples."

"Apples?" said the manager. "We feed our monkeys bananas."

But he brought in a basket of apples. Zelig and the other monkeys polished the apples on their fur and began to munch.

Then Zelig began to pat his head.

"He wants his kippah!" cried Yossi.

"The little hat?" the manager asked, holding out the kippah.

Zelig grabbed it and put it on, hopping back and forth.

"Perhaps now they'll perform," said Yossi.

But the other monkeys started patting their heads too. They all wanted kippahs!

The circus manager moaned. "Where am I going to get eight more little hats?"

Yossi looked in his basket. He had exactly eight kippahs. He handed one to each monkey, and they all did the same hopping dance of delight.

First Zelig, then the others, burst onto the stage, leaping about, swinging through the air, even juggling apples—the kippahs never falling from their heads.

The audience cheered.

But Yossi could only think of how much he would miss Zelig.

"Who makes these wonderful little hats that my monkeys love?" asked the manager.

"My wife," said Yossi. "She also makes vests."

"Could she make eight?" asked the manager.

"Why eight?" asked Yossi. "There are nine monkeys."

The manager sighed. "The one on your shoulder is not happy here anymore. He loves you. You may keep him in return for the vests."

"My wife can sew the vests tonight!"
said Yossi happily.

Zelig rode on Yossi's shoulder all the way home, where Malka sewed vests, shiny and soft, in eight colors.

Yossi and Zelig made a great team. When Shavuot arrived, Yossi had enough rubles to buy flour for challah and cheese for blintzes. And he had enough coins beneath his pillow to buy Shavuot flowers for Malka.

Whenever the circus came to town, Yossi was always in the front row. Zelig would join the show, leaping and flying with the other monkeys in their kippahs and vests.

Then the two friends would head home as the fading light glowed in every color of the rainbow.